CANNIBAL ISLAND

Michael Faun

DYNATOX MINISTRIES

East Brunswick – Borneo – Fisherville

Published by
DYNATOX MINISTRIES
http://dynatoxministries.com

AUTHOR'S NOTE:

In your hands, you're holding the 2nd edition of Cannibal Island, my contribution to Dynatox Ministries's Cannibalsploitation Series. Thank you for purchasing my book! This was originally published as a limited hardcover edition along with three other volumes written by Nick Cato, Jonathan Moon, and Jamie Grefe. I wrote mine between November 2013 and March 2014, on a 19th century Victorian melodrama movie kick. And though this tale is more of a macabre interwar period piece filtered through gaudy EC Comics colors, I hope you find it to your liking.

Enjoy!

Michael Faun, 9/5/15, 12:31 pm

Acknowledgments

Thanks to Dynatox Ministries and Jordan Krall for publishing this book again; Justin T. Coons for the mind-blowing cover art; Nick Cato for eye-lasering away textual mistakes and errors; Philip LoPresti for your kickass comments after reading the story; and Sophia Faun for the original editing and for being the best damn wife in the world!

Love!

Dedicated to every Dynatox-head worldwide

"Dua la kuku halimpati mwewe"
– A chicken's prayer doesn't affect a hawk –
–Swahili Proverb

Prologue
The Gods' Mouth

Abasi's belly was swollen from hunger. Muffled rumblings sounded from inside his empty skin dome as he climbed up a Baobab tree and peered out over the long smooth beach that merged with the black glittering water.

His leathery thumb stroked an oyster shell as he silently prayed for a means with which to feed his famished tribe. He feared they had let down their Gods. Not a sign for months.

A single tear trickled down his sunken cheek as he realized his people were going to die, erased due to the wrath of the higher powers.

Abasi's thoughts were interrupted by something white blinking in the black sky. Small and undulating at first, like a flickering pinprick. But within seconds, it grew to a brightly burning torch, bigger and bigger, until it reached the size of a wild moon catapulting down from the obsidian heaven.

A white fire set the world he knew ablaze, blinding him. Then came the Gods' roars. Like a flock of demon leopards racing down from heaven, the earth thundered and shook under the weight of their heavy paws. Thick smoke rose as they clawed into the ground, devouring the burning Ukindo trees.

Abasi howled and raised his thin arms toward the sky – the long spell of silence was finally broken.

Yet, sadness and confusion weighed heavily upon the tribe. Half of them had succumbed under the violent inferno, and the rest couldn't decipher the Gods' message.

Was it a warning?

Were those still alive blessed or did a grimmer fate await them?

The answers came when the fires calmed.

During the first days of the black rain, Abasi and his tribe found that the Gods had opened a giant mouth in the ground. It whispered the deities' divine tongue through curling smoke. The tribe listened day and night, feeding the holy maw with Ukindo and bones so that it would never go hungry nor cease to lull.

BOOK ONE
England

Michael Faun

1.

Meteorite Dreams

Richard Clayworth glanced at his golden pocket watch as he limped past the mighty stone columns of the south portico, toward the pompous entrance to the British Museum. Late, again. Stiff legged, he shuffled across the spacious hall, marveling over the sunken blue panels with a yellow star in each, before ascending the wide York stone staircase leading to a corridor cluttered with white marble statues and glass exhibition cases.

He sighed and wiped sweat off his forehead, putting on the warmest of smiles as he pressed the brass handle of the nail-studded wooden door, and entered the assembly room. He was met with three pairs of eyes.

"Ah, Professor Clayworth. We had just begun to fear you had been kidnapped by the Snowman," the round-glassed gentleman, Mr Hollingsworth, said with a light-hearted chuckle.

"Terribly sorry I'm late." Clayworth took off his hat and coat, nodding to the man and woman seated at the round conference table. "The cursed leg was slowing me down again." He settled himself into an Oxford leather armchair, smiling at the fair woman who he recognized as Ms. Ramona Fairweather, a geologist like himself, and known for being competitive and fiery. The other face, though, a brittle white haired chap, was new to him. Ms. Fairweather returned a courteous nod.

Mr. Hollingsworth, who stood in front of a large chalkboard, cleared his throat and began to speak while Clayworth helped himself to some tea and biscuits to thaw his frozen bones.

"Now that we are all gathered, I think a brief presentation is in order. But before that, I would like to steal a couple seconds just to say that the British Museum couldn't be more thrilled to have such a skilled team aboard this coming adventure. Such a glorious trio of master academics, whose accumulated expertise in the respective fields of work, would truly turn both Sir Charles Lyell and Doctor Richard Bright green with envy." Hollingsworth's white-bearded face twisted into a sheepish grin.

Quiet laughter came from around the table.

"So… with no further ado. Professor Richard Clayworth, you will lead this expedition as head geologist. You will have the lovely Miss Ramona Fairweather here to assist you. Oh, and Doctor Thomas Wilson," Hollingsworth gestured respectfully to the white-haired gentleman, "decorated with the Victoria Cross for the many lives he saved during the Fourth Anglo-Ashanti War, will operate as your field medical doctor if, God forbid, any exotic bugs should bite you."

Clayworth bowed his head slightly at the doctor, whose stare was strangely glued to the table.

Poor devil! What horrors mustn't he have witnessed? Clayworth's mood dropped for a moment.

"Furthermore," Hollingsworth continued while writing their names on the chalkboard, "an expert on African culture, Christophe Dupont, and a renowned photographer, Finley Mackintyre, will be joining your expedition. Now, I will not take up your valuable time by rambling your extraordinary experience, which I fear would demand you to stay the night. There will be plenty of time for that during the banquet held on the Blue Marlin, the icebreaker which will take you to your destination." Hollingsworth pushed his glasses from the tip of his nose and reached for his cup of tea.

Clayworth, Wilson and Ms. Fairweather replied with polite cheers and a round of quiet applause.

"You will depart from the port of London five days from now, and the banquet shall be held the night before. There, you will meet the two other fellows as well as the Captain. Now to the details. As the letter stated, the meteorite struck one of the unpopulated islands, located about twenty miles off the Zanzibar coast." Hollingsworth drew a crude sketch of the area and then continued. "Here we believe. Right amidst the archipelago…"

Two hours later, the meeting was over. They all rose from their seats and shook hands, rallied up about the coming geological expedition. What might they discover at the meteorite island? Clayworth couldn't have been happier to be assigned an excursion of this importance as his last, before starting his new life, far away from lecturing about rocks and digging into mud.

2.
Shooting Pheasants at the Banquet

Blue Marlin was a fine piece of steam powered machinery. A loyal lady, built to last and dressed in her loveliest nautical gown, ready to host the blessed party of five that constituted the Clayworth Expedition.

The banquet was, of course, held in her mess room. Serving staff bustled about, pouring fine wines and putting forth delicious dishes. There was even a string quartet performing Edward William Elgar's fine pieces while the expedition members dined and conversed around the white cloth table filled with silver trays. A mere slice of the selected gourmet treats included Quails in Pastry, Lobster Merville, Braised Veal, and Rhubarb Flummery with Cornish cream.

"Professor Clayworth, I can already see the cover for *Time Magazine* with yourself standing proudly by the crater, showing the world a slice of space," said Mackintyre, the young boisterous photographer, and carved into his lobster. "And I am thinking, for that kind of picture, I might try my new set of Kalosat Spectral Diffusion Lenses. I can just imagine that picture, it would be quite magnificent." The strong and rather good looking fellow then made the dire mistake of chewing with his mouth open. His crooked front teeth somewhat gave him the look of a rat.

"I am sure it will be a splendid photography, Mr. Mackintyre." Clayworth, whose conversation with Wilson had been interrupted, smiled politely at Mackintyre, sipped from his glass of deep-red Bordeaux and dabbed his mouth with his pearl-white handkerchief. "Now Doctor, you were saying?"

Wilson stared at Mackintyre, appalled at the man's bad table manners, and tried to resume the conversation with Clayworth, that had mostly been about the war. "Oh, yes, Professor. Where was I now...?" Searching for his lost thought, Wilson rubbed his brick chin, when Ms. Fairweather bluntly broke into the conversation.

"So, professor. What do you suppose we will find on the island?" Ms. Fairweather bored her emerald eyes into Clayworth's and slowly let her plump lips embrace the rim of her crystal wine glass. "I certainly hope Mr. Hollingsworth was right about it being unpopulated. I could not bare the thought of some savage undressing me with its wicked eyes," she said and giggled.

Clayworth instantly traced one glass too many in her Yorkshire accent. He cast a quick glance at the expedition's fifth member, the Africa expert, Christophe, who squirmed in his seat from her improper comment. "Ms. Fairweather, to address your last concern first: I am quite sure you have nothing to fear. Christophe knows the area better than the palm of his hand, isn't it so, Christophe?"

"Yes, sir," Christophe answered with an offended grin. His English had a slightly French ring to it. "I grew up on Murago Island." He gently put down his cutlery beside his lobster plate and his spidery fingers traveled to a faint, but clearly visible, scar on his left cheek.

Ms. Fairweather shrank in her red velvet chair. Her eyes were transfixed on the empty plate before her as her freckled skin blushed.

"Now, my dear Ms. Fairweather," Clayworth straightened his back and scooped up a little yolk of quail on his fork with his knife. "To answer your second question, I try not to suppose anything. Supposition, even presumption for that matter, is truly the mother of disappointments." He put the fork into his mouth and savored each chew. "Call me an old geezer, but I detest building my hopes up just to have them shot down like a pheasant in the next moment. I suppose I have learned it the hard way, after some twenty odd years as a geologist." He grinned and wiped his mouth. "Good heavens, doctor. You must try the quail. It is stunning, absolutely stunning."

Ms. Fairweather threw her napkin on her plate and brusquely left the table, leaving a trail of Chanel No.5.

Clayworth and Christophe shared a comradely smile and finished their plates, while listening to Mackintyre trying to persuade the good, but most reluctant, Doctor Wilson to be the object of his next photography. Apparently, it would be called *Portrait of a War Hero*.

3.
Cocktails & Adventures at Sea

The ship's bell rang ten o'clock when Blue Marlin's burly captain finally decided to show his Newgate-fringed face. The members of the expedition, sans Wilson and Christophe, who had retired after the banquet, were joined inside the Green Lounge for evening cocktails when the proud ship-owner tromped into the smoky room, wherein a crackling gramophone played a cheerful medley of Vera Lynn tunes.

"Ah, good evening ladies and gentlemen, I am your captain, Austin Dunkley." He tipped his white cap and the members greeted him. "I notice there are two of you amiss, and I do want to apologize for not introducing myself earlier. I ran into some unexpected difficulties with the harbor master that delayed me. I fear poor old James is losing his memory. Anyhow, it is all sorted out now and I am happy to tell you that we will depart in six hours. If you have any questions, wishes, or anything else for that matter, please let me know how I can be of service." He produced an ivory pipe and a leather tobacco pouch from his deep-blue overcoat.

"Say, Captain." Ms. Fairweather swirled her glass close to her décolletaged black tassel evening gown; a glittery tiara framed her curly copper-red hair. "When do you expect us to get there... to the island?" She ran a finger around the brim of the glass and giggled tipsily. "See, I forgot to pack a book to make time pass quicker, and I do get bored so easily."

Clayworth cleared his throat and cast a reticent glance at the blushing captain, who seemed to buy her playful invite, lock, stock and barrel.

Dunkley lit his pipe with a delighted smile. A plume of thick smoke shrouded his face the next moment, as he addressed Ms. Fairweather with an authoritative, yet soft, tone. "I expect us to reach the Zanzibar coast in twenty days. And I simply refuse to have any of my passengers, let alone a fair lady such as yourself, pestered with tediousness meanwhile. I would be more than happy to let you browse my personal library in my quarter on the bridge deck. But I must warn you," he leaned closer to Ms. Fairweather, his eyes half-closed as he whispered, "you will only find books about my adventures at sea." He burst out in a raspy chuckle and sucked on his pipe.

"Really?" Ms. Fairweather's glassy eyes widened. "That sounds *marvelous*. I love adventures at sea."

Dunkley kissed her hand and winked. "Now, if you'll excuse me, I will leave you to your drinks and music, and bid you all good night." On that note, he withdrew to the captain's quarters, filled with the hopes of late night company.

Close to midnight, Ms. Fairweather danced and hummed along with the Vera Lynn songs, drunk from the several glasses of Champagne she had finished since dinner.

Mackintyre sat cross-legged in one of the lounge's leather armchairs, intensely eyeing Clayworth. "Tell me honestly, professor. How could you be so calm? I mean, doesn't your heart accelerate just a little, when pondering over what could be discovered at the meteorite island? I heard what you told Ms. Fairweather, it's just that... I cannot believe one can be so utterly cool about the matter." He scooped up a handful of nuts from a glass bowl and flipped them into his mouth with the speed of a starved squirrel.

"Mr. Mackintyre, I admire your sense of adventure. I wish I still had my own." Clayworth let out a light-hearted chuckle and took a drag from his cigarette, knocking off ash into a silver tray. Leisurely dressed in a dark waistcoat and Oxford bags, he relaxed in a velvet couch and enjoyed a glass of brandy. "I assume you like to indulge in the various pulp magazines that are bombarding our nation. Am I correct?" He grinned amusedly, took another drag of tobacco and dipped into his drink.

"Guilty," Mackintyre laughed and held up his hands. "And you know, Professor, it is never too late to get lost in some wonder and sensation. We will be stuck on this ship for quite a while... perhaps you would like to borrow one or two for sheer entertainment?" He narrowed his eyes and lowered his hands. "Say, professor, have you ever read Jules Verne's novel, *Off on a Comet*? I like to think that we are on our way to such an adventure."

"The fact that I am nearly fifty years of age does not make me a dull old mummy, whose only interest in life is boulder-scrutinizing and dust-collecting." Clayworth leaned closer and blew out a plume of smoke. "No, Mr. Mackintyre, I have read my share of adventure novels, believe me. But the one you are referring to is *not* cheap pulp, but the work of a

French cuckoo who spent his days making up silly fantasies that corrupts the susceptible brains of your generation."

"Oh..." Mackintyre's face turned blank and he stopped chewing for a moment.

Clayworth emptied his glass. "Yes, you see, as opposed to our own H.G. Wells, Verne had no scientific facts to back his fantasies. I am sorry, lad, but we will not find anything but mud and rocks on that island." He snuffed his cigarette and stretched his back as he stood. "Well, I am going out for some refreshing night air and afterwards I think I will surrender for the evening. It was good to get to know you a little better, Mr. Mackintyre. Now, do not get lost in those pulps of yours. Good night." He grabbed his heavy coat and fur hat, and nodded politely at the preoccupied Ms. Fairweather who didn't seem to notice his leaving the lounge.

4.
Portrait of a War Hero
1901

Inside the feebly lit sick tent, Wilson tried to ignore the dreadful screams coming from the soldier lying on the makeshift bed. The young man had a block of wood logged between his teeth not to crack them during the coming amputation. His infected leg had gone from bad to worse as African mosquitoes had laid eggs in an unattended bullet wound, and now, the hatched larvae had eaten so much of the flesh, it could not be saved.

Wilson wiped sweat off his cheeks with a cloth. He adjusted his glasses and took a steady grip on the bone saw, and initiated the ugly procedure. One could never get used to the sickening sound of metal cutting through bone. And the smell! Sweat, burnt flesh, and putrid pus.

Suddenly, the tent door flapped open. In stepped a stern-faced man with a thin moustache and cold tombstone eyes. Wilson knew him as Officer Hubbart; a feared man among the troops.

"Officer? What is the meaning of this? I am in the middle of a—"

"Doctor Wilson, abort Private Appleton's amputation immediately." Hubbart brusquely barged toward Wilson, whose face twisted into an agitated frown.

"But, Sir, with all due respect, I can't stop now!?"

Hubbart handed Wilson a document while the half amputated Appleton howled with pain, his breathing fast and strained.

"What!?" Appalled, Wilson stared at the paper. "But this is..." His narrowed eyes traveled to Hubbart, who stood looming like a statue over him. "Murder..." Wilson quietly ended his sentence.

Firing rifles echoed in the distance.

"It is an immediate order!" Hubbart yanked the document back. He put it over the flickering flame of the oil lamp and set it ablaze. "You will treat it just like any other order. Strictly confidential. And rest assured, it is in the best interest of the British Empire." Hubbart smirked as the document disintegrated to ash and sprinkled over the tent floor like black snow. He then left Wilson alone with his tormented patient who, according to the document, was a threat to the Empire. A witness of war crime – who therefore must be eliminated.

Gritting his teeth, Wilson doused sweat from Appleton's drenched face. He silently fished out a hypodermic syringe and a bottle of morphine which he drained entirely, thus preparing a lethal dose. He closed his eyes as the needle penetrated his patient's steaming skin, slowly injecting the vile fluid into his patient's bloodstream.

Within a minute, Appleton's scream dwindled to a coughing gargle. His body stopped shaking and turned limp as he finally expired...

"Hubbart!"

Wilson started awake from the high pitched yell. And recognized the voice as his own. Drowsy, he opened his heavy eyelids and saw his own bony fingers in a firm grip around Christophe's throat. The small and gangly assistant gasped for air and struggled to free himself from Wilson's finger shackle.

"Dctrr... plsshh..." Christophe wheezed, his body thrashing wildly.

Suddenly, the cabin door slammed open.

"By Jove, Doctor!" Clayworth shouted as he rushed into Wilson's dimly lit cabin.

Wilson snapped out of his spell and released his lock around Christophe, who, coughing, staggered backwards while stroking his sore finger-imprinted neck. He stared at Wilson with fear in his wide eyes.

"What on earth is going on?" Clayworth hobbled over to Christophe's aid, staring suspiciously at the two men.

"I-I... am so sorry, I was having a horrid nightmare," Wilson mumbled and rubbed his glistening forehead. His eyes were far away.

"What happened, Christophe? What are you doing in the Doctor's room?" Clayworth demanded.

"Sir, I heard the doctor scream. I hurried inside his room thinking he was feeling ill. I saw him having a fit, so I tried to wake him up when he," Christophe swallowed, "suddenly grabbed my neck and called me... Hubbart." Christophe's words came out shaky.

"I'm so sorry, lad." Wilson scratched his balding head. "I do not know what came over me."

"Do not worry, Christophe. Confusion seems to be the only culprit here, to be sure." Clayworth patted Christophe's shoulder. "Please, would you be so kind and fetch the bottle of brandy from my room? I will talk to the good doctor. Oh, and bring two glasses, will you?"

"Of course, sir." Christophe nodded and trotted out of the stateroom. He soon returned with Claworth's requested items and placed them on Wilson's bedside table.

"Thank you, Christophe. Now, try and get some sleep and I will see you in the morrow at breakfast. Good night." Clayworth seated himself in a chair by the bed next to Wilson.

Before Christophe left the room, he cast an apprehensive glance at Clayworth and then at Wilson, who looked ashamed and didn't meet his eyes. "Good night, professor... doctor." He left the cabin and closed the door quietly behind him.

Clayworth poured brandy into the glasses and offered one to Wilson. "Here, this will help you settle your nerves, Doctor." Wilson accepted it with a trembling hand and downed the liquor in one swig.

"Thank you, professor. You are a good-hearted man." Wilson smiled and wiped his lips with the hairy back of his hand. "That poor dark lad. Ha! Must think I've got bats in the belfry," he chortled.

"Oh, do not worry, doctor. Christophe's a good man, too. I am sure he understands you were only having a bad dream." Clayworth had picked up a chemical smell the instant he darted into the room. But it wasn't until now, as things had calmed down, that he noticed the small brown bottle whose label read *Battle & Co Chemist Corporation Papine 12 oz Morphine,* and the syringe lying next to it. He felt a twang of pity – what demons mustn't the good doctor struggle against to turn to that filth?

"Well, I feel much better now, thank you." Wilson put his empty glass on the bedside table.

"I'm glad of it, doctor. Say..." Clayworth narrowed his eyes, "Christophe said you were calling out a name while you were str – during your... spell. Hubbart?"

Wilson's face grew tight. "Hubbart...?"

"Yes. Must be quite an unpleasant fellow to stir up such a reaction?"

"It is odd what the mind can conjure. Never heard that name before in my life," Wilson chuckled. "Must have been a figment of my sleep-deprived imagination."

"I see," Clayworth smiled. "Well, I will leave the brandy here in case you should have another bad dream. I am awfully tired myself and think it best to get back to my own bed and catch some descent sleep before dawn." He emptied his glass and got up with the help of his cane. "Sleep well, doctor."

"And you, professor." Wilson offered a reassuring grin.

On his way out, Clayworth caught a glimpse of the doctor in the large mirror on the wall. A jolt of fright coursed through him as he saw

Wilson's kind wrinkly face twist into a most diabolical expression as he snuggled back down underneath his stale bedclothes.

5.
The Eye of the Wicked Wolf

"Isn't the music simply marvelous?" Ms. Fairweather blissfully sighed and threw herself over a velvet divan close to Mackintyre. "When this little adventure is over, I think I am going to visit Paris. That is where real life is happening. Just imagine it Finley, the grand ballroom dances, the fantastic fashion. Not to mention the French gentlemen!" Ms. Fairweather broke out in a high-pitched drunken giggle.

"Yes, Ms. Fairweather. Paris is indeed a place of beauty. I lived there for three years, actually. Made some wonderful plates there. Say, are you familiar with the avant-garde? I met this amazing fellow, a photographer like myself, Radnitzky I think his name was. Yes, I am quite sure of it. Emmanuel. An American who introduced me to the most interesting artists I have ever met." Mackintyre laughed softly. "Perhaps we could travel there together? I know some enjoyable people and I would be more than happy to show you around to some of the..." His sentence died in favor of Ms. Fairweather's sawmill snoring. Next moment, the ship's bell tolled two o'clock, and along with her heavy sleep, indicated the death of the evening.

Mackintyre popped a final nut into his mouth, finished his drink and stood. He looked at Ms. Fairweather, who reminded him of a sleeping angel, her copper hair flowing out over the green velvet divan-bed. His innocent stare grew lewd. His eyes wandered to her smooth, milk-toned thighs, now partially exposed as her tassel dress had slipped up against the shiny couch. He bit his lip and steered his gaze the other way.

"Oh, behave Finley," he silently mouthed and gently pulled down her dress to a length of decency. He shoved his arms in under her neck and knees and lifted her. He carried her from the lounge and into the corridor, where Ms. Fairweather's cabin was, next to his own. But just outside her door he hesitated and reasoned it was better to let her wear out the drunken spell on the couch in his own room. That way, he could supervise her and avoid the risk of her vomiting in her sleep.

It is the gentleman thing to do! Mackintyre thought as he used his elbow to open his door. He squinted as he stepped into the darkness and shambled over to the studded Chesterfield sofa, on which he carefully lay her down. He flicked a switch, and a violet-shaped table lamp in the corner sparked up a soft purple glow which slowly spread inside the oak wood-paneled stateroom.

Next, as he drew a blanket over her, he accidentally brushed his hand against her ample bosom and recoiled from fear of waking her, or rather, that she should wake and get the wrong idea that he was molesting her in her sleep. Ms. Fairweather didn't even flinch. All those drinks had made her sleep like a log, and for all he knew, she was probably in a state of semi-unconsciousness by now. Still, the touch of her soft skin against his had sent a bolt of pleasure to between his legs, and his member was growing rigid as the forbidden thoughts burgled his stirring mind.

Breathing heavily, he peered over at his camera equipment that was stacked against the corner. Guilty excitement washed over him, and it must have been either some dark force, or the Devil, that made him unbutton the upper part of her black gown. Gingerly, and with his eyes locked on hers so that he could anticipate any unwanted reaction.

None came.

Mackintyre felt like the big bad wolf as he deftly set up his tripod and mounted his camera on it. He moved the purple lamp closer to his object, until he had found the perfect light in which to portray Ms. Fairweather's full and bare, chalk-white breasts.

6.
A Clandestine Agreement

Christophe woke to the sound of distant gunshots coming from the upper deck. He washed up and got dressed, his throat still hurting after the nightly incident in Wilson's cabin. The failed strangle attempt had stirred up an ugly memory from his childhood, one when he was barely seven years old. One traumatic night, his father had suffered a drunken delirium. Convinced that his own son was the evil spirit *Tokoloshe*, he had stormed into Christophe's room wielding a big knife, screaming madly as he sliced the boy's chin. Bleeding profusely, and scared out of his wits, he had managed to fend him off. The father's assault continued on his mother as Christophe fled out into the night. When he returned at dawn, he had found her lifeless on the floor, strangled to death. He could still hear the tinkling sound of the bottle he sent shattering over his sleeping father's head.

Christophe wrapped his wool coat tighter around him. A dark cloud stooped over him as he ascended the metal staircase to the sun deck.

"Pull!" Mackintyre's shrill voice echoed through the chilled air. The next moment a loud bang resounded, and was followed by a round of applause.

The glaring winter sun hit Christophe's eyes as he walked out the glass door. Just as he had thought, clay pigeon shooting was the morning's curriculum. By the gunwale stood Mackintyre, armed with a rifle aimed toward the air. He was flanked by Captain Dunkley who stood smoking his pipe while operating the thrower. Professor Clayworth cheerfully laughed as he chatted with the ruddy captain.

They had left the English Channel and were now out on open water, a floor of ice, steadily cracking underneath. Christophe's grim mood soon dissipated as he gazed out over the glistening winterscape that sparkled in the high sun. Frozen air smelling of brine filled his lungs as he smilingly headed toward the group of men.

Clayworth picked up the sound of Christophe's studded boots against the metal floor, and swiveled to face him. "Ah, good morning, Christophe!" He offered a leather-gloved hand and his rosy-cheeked face twisted to a toothy grin.

"Morning, lad." Dunkley raised his pipe in acknowledgement.

"A *beautiful* morning!" Christophe returned. "Such a stunning view. But freezing cold, too!" He hugged himself in jest, clacking his teeth.

"Pull!" Mackintyre yelled again, too engrossed in the target practice to even notice the arrival of the assistant.

Dunkley pulled the lever–

BANG!

–and sent another clay pigeon to its death.

Clayworth tottered closer to Christophe. "I need to share a few words with you. In private," he whispered and shot the assistant a serious face, gently pulling him aside.

"Have I done something wrong, sir?" Christophe frowned, anxious as they walked side by side along the deck and soon passing one of the ship's two majestic funnels.

"Oh, no. Certainly not!" Clayworth chuckled and patted his assistant's shoulder. "No, I wanted to talk with you about last night. Or rather, *about* Doctor Wilson."

"Yes? Is everything alright with him?"

"I fear that it might not be." Clayworth let out a burdensome sigh. "I suspect the poor old fellow is addicted to a certain poison... morphine to be precise." He glanced at Christophe with worry in his stark duke-blue eyes.

"Morphine, sir?" Christophe returned a curious look.

"Yes, I fear so. I saw a bottle and a syringe on his bedside table. Now, I need you to keep an eye on him, especially when we arrive at the island. I will not be able to tend to anything but my job at hand while there." Clayworth rubbed his chin thoughtfully. "And we cannot risk the doctor being out of his own game should something happen, god forbid. But please, keep this to yourself. The least we need is to alarm the others."

"Yes, of course, sir." Christophe nodded understandingly.

"Jolly good." Clayworth grabbed Christophe's arm and squeezed it firmly. "I am pleased to have you aboard this expedition. Honest and loyal men are a rare breed nowadays. Now, let us enjoy a steady breakfast. I believe my stomach just cried for some tea and crumpets."

On that note, the two men headed back to Dunkley and Mackintyre, after which all four of them ventured down to the galley, guided by the welcoming scent of freshly baked bread.

7.
Of Tektite & Desires

When Ms Fairweather woke she didn't recognize the room she was in. Her mouth was dry and tasted of decayed grapes. On top of that, her skull banged horribly.

She sat up in the Chesterfield sofa she was lying on. As she smoothed out her disheveled hair, vague flashes from last night resurfaced like pictorial tidal waves. The embarrassments piled up one another like corpses in a mass grave – stinking and all over the place.

She looked around the room and noticed a camera sitting on a tripod in the corner.

What on earth am I doing in Mackintyre's stateroom?

Her heart plummeted in her chest as her hands instinctively felt her knickers and bra and found that both garments were corrupt and askew.

Oh no, what an absolute mess! First night aboard and I have already behaved like an utter tart…

Anxiety-ridden, Ms. Fairweather staggered out of the young – *much too young* – photographer's cabin and scurried into her own quarter next to his.

A long hot shower and a bracer later, she had managed to wash away almost all of the sleaze-coating she felt covered in. All she needed now was to make some social repairs, and then it would be alright again. She drained her second White Lady and forced a smile. She stepped out of her red silk Kimono and looked at her naked body in the mirror. Her luxuriant breasts were like two perfectly sculptured orbs. Her hips and waist like a streamlined hourglass of flesh. She couldn't grasp, nor accept, that Clayworth didn't seem to notice this. The mere thought of him, his big blue eyes boring into hers while firmly gripping her dainty hand, sent a stream of tingles from her neck and down to her female regions.

Her desire for the handsome professor inflated inside her like a hot balloon. She closed her glazed eyes and gently began stroking the orange tuft of hair covering her sex. A moment later, she lay spread over the bed, pleasing herself imagining Clayworth thrusting his stiff member into her as if his life depended on it. Before long, a pink flower of ecstasy bloomed inside her as she reached climax.

Her body was still trembling as she stepped into a deep-mauve chiffon dress and a pair of amethyst silk stockings. She put on a sparkling bead necklace, a spray of Chanel perfume, and stepped out into the corridor; startling as a figure emerged on her threshold. "Professor," Ms. Fairweather gasped and clutched at her heart.

"By Jove!" Clayworth flinched and nearly fell from the shock of the door suddenly opening as he was about to knock.

Clayworth and Ms. Fairweather broke out in nervous unison laughter.

"You nearly scared me out of my wits!" Ms. Fairweather rolled her eyes and sighed dramatically. "You mustn't sneak up on ladies like that."

"I am truly sorry, Ms. Fairweather. It was certainly not my intention to give you a fright." Clayworth steadied himself with his cane, arching a brow. "I simply came to call on you since you deprived us of your presence during luncheon. We almost began to worry you had grown tired of the humdrum company of men and rowed back to London in one of the lifeboats."

"Oh, professor, do not be silly. If somebody ought to row away from here it would certainly be one of you fellows, who had to suffer my improper behavior last night." Ms. Fairweather blushed and offered a demure smile. "I have not a clue what got into me. Please accept my apology, professor."

"It is quite alright. We have all had a drink too many on occasion. Myself included." Clayworth raised his hand and put on a charming smile. "Now that I have you on the hook, though, would you care to join me in my cabin? I have some work details I thought we should go over."

Ms. Fairweather's heart jolted. She could literally feel her pulse climb. "Why, of course, professor. I would like nothing more."

"Splendid!" Clayworth beamed. "This way, then." Like a true gentleman, he looped his elbow, and arm-in-arm they trotted toward his stateroom located on larboard. Ms. Fairweather pranced onward with her head held high, fancying herself *Mrs. Clayworth;* a title that rang nicely indeed.

As they reached the door to Clayworth's stateroom he suddenly turned and faced Ms. Fairweather. "I have something to confess–" he began and stared deep into her eyes. Her pupils dilated and her cheeks felt hot. Was this the moment she had been waiting for? A proposal?

She inched closer, "Oh, have you, professor?"

Clayworth gently took her hand. "Ms. Fairweather... I am quite excited, so please forgive my blunt manners..." He cleared his throat. "I do not know how to put this but–"

"–Yes?"

Clayworth hesitated, and then whispered softly into her warm ear, "I believe there is a great chance of finding Tektites at the site."

BOOK TWO
Zanzibar

Michael Faun

8.
Quandaries

"Have a look, Ms. Fairweather." Clayworth handed over his binoculars to Ms. Fairweather, who stood next to him on the bow. She aired her white blouse, and through the looking glass saw the lush island that looked like a fantasy paradise with large swaying palms and a sprawling beach. The island was sheltered by sandy spots and dry bushes emerging from the bright turquoise water that glittered in the blazing sun. The warm breeze carried a sweet herbal smell, and she made the curious notion that a black smoke pillar was curling from behind the immense shield of tropical trees which covered the island. "Why, that's odd, professor... how come it is–"

"Smoking? Yes, I am quite intrigued by the strange fact myself. Might be pulverized rock, perhaps even melted biotite. We will get the answers as soon as we find a way to embark on the damn island." Clayworth's tone was edgy. He wiped sweat off his furrowed brows and tapped his cane irritably.

"It is marvelous..." Ms. Fairweather dreamily whispered.

"It is ridiculous!" Clayworth blustered. "Three weeks of wearisome traveling, only to find that we cannot pass through the cursed archipelago on account of this hefty harlot of a boat!?"

Dunkley arrived to the bow just in time to pick up Clayworth's acidic, and awfully loud, comment. He gritted his teeth and retorted, "Please, calm down, Mr. Clayworth. I assure you I have tried my utmost to sort out this unfortunate situation and I guarantee you, there is nothing I can do about it. You will have to use the lifeboats and row the last stretch to the island. I cannot risk taking her along these shallow waters. And as the captain of this... *harlot*, I simply refuse to push her even an inch further." He sucked coolly on his pipe and squinted at Clayworth.

"Oh well," Clayworth sighed. "We had better start loading the boats then." He stroked his forehead absent-mindedly. "I hope you can forgive my harsh choice of words, captain. I did not mean to insult you, nor your fine vessel. Blue Marlin is nothing but a first class lady. It is just... well, not being out on the field for three long weeks drives me completely mad."

Ms. Fairweather lowered the binoculars and grinned. "The professor is right, captain. Sadly, this goes for all of our kind. Us hopeless mud-diggers, that is."

Dunkley blew a plume of smoke, his fat lips curving upwards till they almost reached his hairy ears. "Apology accepted, professor. I am quite aware that your kind is not built for a life on the sea." He broke out in a hearty chuckle and patted Clayworth's shoulder. "I will fetch my crew so they can load your effects. Meanwhile, you should start packing and gather your members up here on deck." He turned to Ms. Fairweather and tipped his cap with a flirtatious wink. "Miss, if you do not mind I would be more than happy to row you there myself."

Ms. Fairweather blushed at the polite offer. Her chin, as well as generous chest, rose with self-esteem. "Oh, not at all, captain. How considerate of you." She cracked a delighted smile, offering her hand.

Dunkley, who nearly dropped his meerschaums pipe in surprise, quickly kissed her hand before he plodded away, humming a sprightly sea shanty. "It's of a brisk young lively lad, came out of Gloucestershire, and all his full intention was to court a lady fair. Her eyes they shone like morning dew..."

"Well, I suppose we do best by following the captain's order." Clayworth snickered. His before sullen spirit now seemed lifted as he and Ms. Fairweather ambled below deck. In the corridor, they bumped into Mackintyre and Christophe, each wearing inquisitive expressions.

"Professor! What is going on?" Mackintyre's wondered. "Why is the ship standing still?"

"And we are still on the water. Is there a problem?" Christophe filled in.

"Gentlemen." Ms. Fairweather brushed past them and headed to her stateroom.

"Please, settle down, fellows. There is absolutely no reason for alarm." Clayworth fished up his golden pocket watch and glanced at it before facing them again. This time with cunning eyes and a warm smile. "But I sure hope you young and able men are up for a little morning exercise. Tell me, Mackintyre, how well versed are you in the art of rowing?"

Mackintyre and Christophe exchanged baffled looks.

"I will explain soon enough. Pack your bags and meet me up on deck within the hour. Meanwhile, I will go and wake the lie-abed doctor, whom I notice is not with you. Oh, and I almost forgot. Have a look at the meteorite island." Clayworth snickered as he, too, walked straight through them and made the royal wave just before disappearing around the corner to Wilson's cabin.

Tok. Tok. Tok, Clayworth softly tapped his cane on Wilson's door.

Not a sound.

Damn you if you have used that horrible poison again! Clayworth's stomach knotted from the mere thought of finding Wilson out of his wits. Even worse was the idea of the others finding out that the expedition's only physician was in fact an unreliable drug fiend. He gritted his teeth and prayed it was not so.

"Doctor...?" He put his ear against the wood. Not even a snore. "I am truly sorry to disturb your sleep, but we have arrived now."

A bolt of dread coursed through Clayworth as he picked up an unsettling creaking coming from inside the doctor's room.

"Wilson!? Are you there?"

As there was still no answer, Clayworth decided to break the rules of privacy. His pulse climbed as he carefully pressed the door handle and peered through the chink into the dark room. "No!" he gasped, and hobbled toward Wilson's limp body that dangled in a waist belt from the lamp in the ceiling.

9.
Meteorite Island

Frolicking dolphins rode the bow of the two lifeboats that moved toward shore in a slow but steady pace. The gaiety of the bottlenoses, adding the spectacular weather and view, contrasted morbidly against the somber atmosphere of the dismayed expedition members.

"What an absolutely dreadful way to end one's life. Poor, poor Doctor Wilson." Ms. Fairweather leaned against a boat pillow in the stern. Her face was etched in a disturbed frown and she stared at a group of black Herons soaring above them. "Do you believe in ghosts, captain?"

"Why, yes of course, miss!" Dunkley's face was serious. "I have witnessed many a ghost in my life."

Ms. Fairweather broke her listless bird watching and looked at the captain with wide eyes. "Really?"

"Yes. Last week at the very latest, when young Mackintyre insisted on having a try of my pipe... I suppose I should have warned him I had stuffed it with a quart of extra strong Turkish Delight." Dunkley chuckled and stroked the oars with more force. Despite his attempt at a joke, his spirits were low.

Ms. Fairweather laughed quietly. "I appreciate your easing my mind, captain. You have a kind heart." She received a gentle smile in return.

The other boat was dead silent. Clayworth, lost in thoughts, sat leaned against a wooden field desk between Christophe and Mackintyre, who, amid the generous pile of luggage, struggled to row the slightly overtaxed boat.

Minutes before their departure, Dunkley had radioed the British authorities, who had ordered for Doctor Wilson's body to be brought back to England for an honorable military funeral. This, unfortunately, meant that time was now cut to fine and instead of the planned ten days, the expedition would only have two – something that heavily jeopardized the scientific outcome.

The stretch to the meteorite island had taken about thirty minutes, and it was early afternoon when they finally set up their base camp on the white powdery sand beach that swarmed with hermit crabs poking around the driftwood. Dunkley had helped them unload before he returned to the Blue Marlin who lay anchored out by the bay.

"I will prepare for afternoon tea and a light lunch. Food is always good remedy for a blackened heart." Christophe announced to the group and produced several cans of sausage and beans from a wooden box. He looked at them, weighing the alternatives for the meal while Ms. Fairweather was heard rooting around in her canvas tent, and Mackintyre plodded around the beach, whistling and taking photos.

"Thank you, Christophe." Clayworth put down the notebook he was perusing. "You are right, even the cursed need to eat. I just cannot seem to shake off the haunting feeling that I should have done something."

Christophe lit the field stove and took a swig of water, glancing at Clayworth. "It was not your fault, sir. There is an African saying: Only a goat that is tired of life, invites a lion to dinner."

Clayworth shot Christophe a curious look. "What does it mean?"

Christophe removed the can of heated water from the stove and poured it into a tea pot. "That Doctor Wilson would have put an end to his life sooner or later anyway."

Clayworth frowned and stood up, sniffing as a pleasant citrus aroma spread over the camp; strong enough to lure the fair sex out of her little hut.

"Oh, tea!" Ms. Fairweather cooed. "How lovely!" She was rubbing mosquito ointment onto her arms as she approached the others. She had changed her clothes to attires more suitable for field work: a pair of khaki trousers and a light shirt, sturdy boots, and a jaunty pith helmet.

"Oh, Ms. Fairweather." Clayworth greeted while stirring his reeking tea. "How are you getting along?"

"Here you are, miss." Christophe smiled and handed her a cup.

"Thank you, Christophe." A faint smile stirred her lips as she accepted the hot beverage and faced Clayworth. "I am fine, thanks, professor. Say, where is Mr. Mackintyre?"

"Oh, he was here just now..." Clayworth arched a brow as he peered over the beach. "But it seems he has wandered off on an excursion of his own."

10.
A Venture Into the Wild

Mackintyre felt just like one of the adventuring characters from his favorite novel, Sir H. Rider Haggard's *King Solomon's Mine,* as he explored the island's magnificent views through the eye of his camera. The variety of shades and contrasts of the exotic trees, plants and bushes, was so vibrant and so spectacular, that the photographs would guarantee to earn him a quid or two when he got back home to England. And yet, the crater was still to be seen.

This sure beats the monotonous, three-week imprisonment aboard that icebreaker.

The Zanzibar heat baked him like a tomato roasted in the oven, slowly – and cruelly – wringing every drop of fluid from his body. He paused for awhile, searching for a shadowy spot to cool down, when he realized he had been so captured by his surroundings, he had traipsed a long way from the camp and whirled straight into the deep vegetation. The air here was thick and moist. Yellow and orange butterflies surrounded him, and stark green birds flitted high up among the treetops as he sat under a canopy of big palm leafs, feeling the heat gradually roll off his sweaty skin.

He looked around the clearing and made a discovery that tickled his curiosity. Shards of broken shell from a giant tortoise and bones, most likely from smaller apes, lay scattered not far from his boots. He moved closer and picked up a piece of the hard shell, when a sudden rustle startled him. He spun around, gasping. His adrenaline spiked and his heart skipped a beat as he pictured a feral Leopard lurking in the thicket.

A creature suddenly jumped out from behind a large bush. Mackintyre recoiled, feeling his heart catapulting out of his chest. Their eyes locked for a brief moment and the meter-high vulture, with red patches around its yellow eyes, shrieked and ruffled up its giant white-black plumage in defense just before it fled for its life, flapping and thrashing through a waxy-leaved aisle.

He let out a strained laugh and clutched at his chest from the shock. Pulling himself together, he brought the camera to his eyes once more, directing it toward the escaping beast of a bird. With trembling hands, he adjusted the sharpness of the lens and held the camera as still as he could. As he watched the vulture take off into the air, he spotted something that made his blood curdle a second time. For up in a leafy tree not five yards away, crouched a tangle-haired native whose dark skin was streaked with dried blood and soot. He stared at Mackintyre through glazed pink eyes while thumbing a necklace of what appeared to be stringed human teeth. A crude spear was held in the wildman's other hand, adorned with molten leaves and a small yellowed skull.

Mackintyre staggered backwards. His eyes were still locked on the native's – he did not dare to break eye-contact in fear of being pierced by the vile spear. The fear came in shockwaves, slowly but steadily gripping him. He felt like prey in the eyes of a jungle cat. Was not the island supposed to be unpopulated? If so, then who in God's name was this? Were there more of these sinister wilds around? Either way, Mackintyre did not feel eager to stick around and find out. After his fifth retraced step he swallowed, turned, and ran.

Clayworth stared restlessly at his pocket watch. He jabbed his cane into the white sand and drew random patterns. "Unbelievable! We have little, if any, time to study the crater which lies half a day away, and that whippersnapper Finley is out on his own photographic expedition. Two hours and fifteen minutes has he stolen. *Thus far.* Such arrogance!" He flicked up a portion of sand that disintegrated in the air.

"Look, sir!" Christophe pointed his finger toward the orange-glazed fringe a hundred yards away, where the smooth beach curved.

Clayworth snapped out of his spell of frustration and peered in the pointed direction.

"What is it, professor?" Ms Fairweather rose from her beach chair and removed her round sunglasses, adjusting her pith hat not to be blinded by the glaring sun.

"Hand me the binoculars would you, Ms. Fairweather." Clayworth held out his hand, eyes still locked on the sand-shrouded figure in the distance. He received the hot brass field glasses and brought them to his eyes. "By Jove!"

"Is something wrong, sir?" Christophe's voice wore a hint of worry.

"Not sure, Christophe, but he seems scared out of his wits!" Clayworth watched the boisterous photographer run toward the camp like a scalded dog; constantly checking his back as he stumbled through the heavy sand and wheeling his arms as if being chased by a pack of ghosts. "Why, he appears to be chased!"

"Chased!?" Christophe's pulse climbed as he hurried into his tent to fetch the only rifle brought with them. As he came back, the lost photographer just returned.

"Oh, my!" Ms Fairweather dashed over to the fatigued Mackintyre who sank down and collapsed on the sand right outside her tent.

"This island... it is... we are not alone," Mackintyre panted as he lay on his back, sweating profusely. "We must leave... there are savages... I saw one in the tree... "

"Dear Lord!" Clayworth hobbled over to Ms Fairweather who kneeled next to Mackintyre. "Christophe, bring some water, hurry!"

Christophe rushed back into his tent and picked up a canteen of water. With that in one hand, and the loaded Martini Rook rifle in the other, he hurried out and joined the others. He threw a cursory glance over where Mackintyre had emerged into sight and was relieved to see no living thing. He put his hand on Mackintyre's burning forehead. "Sir, he is delusional. I think he is suffering from a fever. These islands are full of pests that could cause such a thing."

Clayworth nodded and pointed his cane at Mackintyre's tent. "Get him inside."

"I am not crazy! I know what I saw! The savage was right there in the tree. He was covered in blood... and... and he had a spear!" Mackintyre protested while being helped to his feet by Ms Fairweather and Christophe.

"There, Mr. Mackintyre, calm down now." Clayworth patted his shoulder as they paced toward the tent. "You will feel better after some rest. We have all been exposed to unhealthy doses of stress lately." He raised his brows at Christophe, who returned a tight-lipped smile. "It is perfectly natural to imagine things, even hallucinate, under these harsh conditions. It is better you stay in your tent while we head out to the site. Documentation can wait till tomorrow."

Mackintyre drank greedily from the canteen and wiped his mouth afterwards. "But, Professor, I swear... I–"

"You heard what Christophe said," Clayworth cut him off. "These parts teem with insects of all sorts. Tics, parasites, probably even poisonous centipedes for all we know. It was foolish of you to venture into the thicket on your own. Let that be a lesson for now and we will all gather later tonight for supper." He waved his cane dismissively and started to pack his tools.

Ms. Fairweather helped Mackintyre into the tent and into bed after which Christophe exposed him to a plethora of curious, and rather smelly, ointments and insect repellants.

Within an hour, the expedition, now reduced to a meager trio, set off toward the smoking crater situated in the middle of the large island, behind the rough and lush, peregrine woods.

11.
Buried in Ash

Heavy breathing and the machete cutting through wiry wood, were the only sounds that had come from the triumvirate during the two hours it had taken to plod through the exotic thicket. The last two-hundred yards or so, the wild chlorophyll, with its chirping and buzzing from insects, suddenly grew to a depressing black-gray wasteland. Here, the lively droning was conspicuous by its absence and the charred trees, gnarled and oddly bent, reminded of decayed twisting fingers. The air was stifling and filled with ash that tumbled around and made it difficult to breathe. It also reduced their vision to a sooty fog.

Pausing for a moment, they all shared a canteen of water to wet their parched throats. They soaked cloths with which to cover their grimy faces before proceeding the final distance; making them look like a band of Bedouins that trudged through a desert of ash. A few minutes later, they were standing by the jagged brim and stared in awe at the mighty crater that opened up before them like a colossal smoldering pit.

"Absolutely stunning," Ms. Fairweather whispered under her breath. She walked along the black rim and proudly stretched out her arms as if she were standing on top of the world. "Now I regret that we did not bring Mackintyre, or at least his camera," she chuckled.

Clayworth, too, bubbled with excitement. "Tell me this was not worth that excruciating hike, Christophe!" He put down his fitted leather tool case and squeezed the assistant's shoulder, suppressing a childish giggle. "It is like a giant bowl of surprises!"

"A pit of smoking coal?" Christophe chuckled and shook his head. "Sir, to tell you the truth, I would prefer to lie in a boat and catch some of the local fish." He winked jokingly and unfolded a small field table, on which he placed Clayworth's assorted tools in perfect order.

Clayworth and Ms. Fairweather laughed at the humorous reply and began their pottering about by browsing the outer depression. This section consisted mainly of large angular rock fragments interspersed with black bubbly metal slag, each about the size of a child's clenched fist. It took them about an hour and a half to work their way toward the centre of the crater; a sea of glowing coal beneath a thick layer of silvery ash. No doubt the most challenging and hazardous section to dig into.

Christophe functioned as a shuttle service, running up and down, aiding the two engrossed geologists with water, tools, and sample jars.

"Any luck yet, Ms. Fairweather?" Clayworth called from the other side of the crater. He had taken a brief pause due to the immense heat and was studying a reddish stone, scribbling down notes from where he stood on the cinder carpet.

"Hardly! Only amphibolites and anatexis." Her words came out exhausted. "And I stumbled upon some rocks containing amygdules, nothing of interest, really. What about you, Professor?"

"Well, much the same on this side." A metallic plunk came as Clayworth dropped the rosy stone into a sample jar. "However, I am quite intrigued by the ever ceasing heat. How much time has passed since the impact? Seven, eight weeks?" He squatted and cut his spade into the hot black sludge, squinting at the viscous matter. "Is it not peculiar that there are no traces of microcrystallines, yet, the crater will not cease its hot activity?"

Suddenly, amid the goo on his shovel, he spotted an unfamiliar chunk of metal the size of a cricket ball. Pointy and black, it wore glinting streaks of deep blue and oozed with steam. Clayworth's heart literally skipped a beat with excitement and his hands began to tremble. "Ms. Fairweather, come quick! Christophe, bring a big jar! Hurry!"

Ms. Fairweather ceased her monotonous spade-poking and hurried over to Clayworth. As did Christhophe, who jogged down from the field table where he had been labeling samples. Their eyes widened as they stared at the mysterious object that rested on the shovel.

"Amazing!" Ms. Fairweather pulled down her cloth and swallowed, her flustered face nearly bursting with glee. "I have never seen anything like it... what could it be?" Her curious eyes glittered as they met Clayworth's.

"I am not certain, Ms. Fairweather." Clayworth carefully picked up the heavy object with large tweezers and admired it with conquer beaming in his narrowed blue eyes. "But I can bet my career that this unique specimen alone is worth an entire field day."

"Really?" Ms. Fairweather inched closer to Clayworth. "Wow."

"Now, you know I am not too keen to jump the gun, but if this odd little beauty is in any way connected to the sensational heat source we are standing amid... it might just have saved our entire expedition!" Clayworth let out a joyous laughter. "Jar, please."

Christophe immediately provided him with one and Clayworth gently dropped the thrilling object into the sample container. "Such a lucky turn!"

"Oh, indeed, professor," Ms. Fairweather joined in and suddenly hugged Clayworth, who nearly lost his balance from the surprise. "Oh, this is almost *too* exciting!"

"Treat this with the same care as you would a newborn child." Clayworth winked at Christophe and handed him the jar.

"Of course, sir." Christophe carefully accepted it with a warm smile and gazed south at the scarlet horizon, whose hue was slowly deepening. "We should head back to the camp before dark. The nocturnal creatures around here are not as friendly as the ones we've got back in England."

"Very well, then, I am more than content with today's work. Let us pack up and be on our way." Clayworth nodded at Ms. Fairweather and shook Christophe's hand. "You have done a terrific job, both of you."

The three expeditioners made cheerful small talk as they ascended the sloping crater. High spirited, they gathered their gear and secured the samples in a close-fitted case. Thus began the long hike back through the cloying two-faced thicket.

12.
A Sultry Night in Zanzibar

Clayworth lay in his tent bed and stared at the ceiling. Suffering from yet another bout of insomnia, his eyes were peeled on a bug of rather disconcerting size that crept along the canvas. Despite this tiresome wakefulness which derived mainly from the exciting discovery earlier that day, there was also a trace of anxiety. Perhaps it was the shock of the doctor's horrid suicide that still clung to him like a needy ape, but after further mulling, he knew it was the fact that this expedition was going to be his last.

He took a deep breath, closed his eyes, and as darkness enveloped his vision, imagination escaped through its prison bars and climbed the walls of his frail mind. In his fantasy he was walking along dimly lit alleyways and twisting streets, but soon got lost in the maze-like design. Echoing laughter clapped through the low tanned tunnels he passed, and thick strong hashish smoke flowed about his feet like a London fog. He stopped by a curious gateway. It was beautifully adorned with dreamlike mystical lozenges, stars and crescents. A woman, fully naked save for a blood-red hijab, slowly emerged on the stairways beyond the gate. She stared at him with alluring black eyes that seemed to swirl with desire. Her breasts were ample with skin-texture smooth like the finest Moroccan silk, and large, mocha-toned areolas encircled the erect nipples which she gently caressed without breaking her intent gaze. Clayworth let go and melted through the gate, and into her...

His lucid dream was interrupted by the swishing sound of his tent-flap opening. He gasped as he saw a slender figure entering his dark hut. He shot right up in his bed and instinctively reached for his cane. "Who...?" The intruder's face suddenly came familiar as a thin stripe of moonlight seeped in. "Ms. Fairweather...? What are—"

"Ssshh..." Ms Fairweather put a finger over her glistening lips as she moved toward his bed like a milk-white feline. She was naked, her chest ample just like that of the woman in his fantasy. Though Ms. Fairweather lacked the facial veil, her red flowing hair reminded slightly of it; enough to fuel his imagination to the point where she could be the mysterious woman beyond the gate.

Clayworth's mouth was half open as she approached him. He swallowed as his drowsy eyes took in her voluptuous body, which was now so close that he could even discern the wetness of her fiery-tufted sex. This aroused him furiously.

He winced from the softness of her moist skin as she zealously straddled him. A dull smell of cherry wine oozed from her warm breath. He reached up and firmly pulled her hair. She arched her back in response and let out a stifled moan. Then he pressed his member deeper into her slick Yorkshire rose and let himself go – just like in the dream...

13.
Caught on Lens

"Move a little to the left, Christophe. And you Ms Fairweather, rest the spade over your shoulder... Great! Professor, raise the stone into the air, it will add a magnificent dramatic effect to the picture." Mackintyre wagged his finger. His arm shot out from the black cloth of the sweltering camera house that was rigged at the bottom of the crater, at the spot of yesterday's discovery. Each of the tripod legs had been placed in a canteen of water so that they would not catch fire.

"Would it not be better if I held one arm around Ms. Fairweather?" Clayworth interposed.

"Yes, that is a splendid idea! Now, stand perfectly still and wear your proudest looks. Remember, the camera picks up every little detail." Mackintyre squinted through the brilliant eye of the 12" Dagor. This composition, wherein the mid-day sun beamed down on the expedition like a giant spotlight where they stood together on the black cinder stage, huddled together in the giant amphitheatre of a crater, surrounded by curtains of tumbling ash, was going to be his pièce de résistance. As his thumb hovered over the trigger, he imagined this picture on the front page of every major newspaper in Britain.

"Say meteorite!" Mackintyre said with a self-confident smile and squeezed the shutter-bulb. But as the word was spoken in unison, accompanied by the characteristic click, something unwanted came into view and was caught on the film.

"Oh my God, there is another one!" Mackintyre suddenly gasped. His face turned pale and he yanked the dark-cloth off his head and pointed over the shoulders of the posing members, up at the high rim of the crater.

"What on earth are you talking about?" muttered Clayworth as they all turned their heads, baffled to see a dark naked woman up there who stared curiously back at them. The sense of surprise snowballed when three more tribal-looking bystanders emerged out of nowhere. Then five, ten, fifteen, and within a minute, what must have been at least three dozen of those vile-looking strangers stood by the crater's rim. Men and women, armed with crude weapons such as spears and machetes. They wore the same homely fashion: a tiny hide-flap that barely – and in some cases not at all – covered their genitals. Some, perhaps those of higher rank, wore masks of what looked like flayed monkey-heads.

"Dear Lord, is that *blood* they are covered in?" Ms. Fairweather's pulse rocketed. She crinkled her pointy nose and fished up her red handkerchief and wrapped it around her face not to breathe in more of the sooty air.

Clayworth laid his hand on Ms. Fairweather's lower back. "Do not worry, dear, they are most likely a friendly sort of tribe, curious of our presence here. And that red color is surely just pigment from a plant." He turned to Christophe, whose face was ridden with concern, and quietly demanded, "Christophe, what is the meaning of this? You were certain that this island was unpopulated, were you not? For I suppose the nocturnal creatures you mentioned before have not slipped out earlier?"

Mackintyre was rapidly packing his equipment and cast worried glances at the primitives above.

Christophe shrugged, shaking his head. "I-I have no clue, Sir! It is very strange. This island has not a single record of tribe presence since the early eighteenth century! I apologize..."

"Could they be... *dangerous?*" Ms. Fairweather whispered, her eyes wandering around the high rim. "I mean, they look so... so threatening."

"Please, Ms. Fairweather, no cause for alarm. We are Britons for heaven's sake!" Clayworth stepped in front of her, leaned closer to Christophe and cleared his throat. "Christophe, go and respectfully tell them that we are busy as bees down here, and that their presence – even though we respect and honor their naturally called-for curiosity – is a tad distracting at the moment." He rubbed his pearled chin and looked down, thinking hard for a second, then raised his index finger. "Oh, and make sure to say that we are *more* than happy to give them a guided tour of the ship as soon as we are done here tomorrow morning."

Christophe hesitated and then said, "Eh, yes of course, sir." He handed the rifle that was slung around his shoulder to Clayworth, and paced toward the northern slope that now teemed with natives. During this silent and slightly daunting walk, he made sure not to look any of them in the eye. He had no clue what this tribe was, but he hoped they were nothing like those who so often appeared in the old stories told by the Tumbatu village elders. With each step, his heartbeats intensified. Could those old myths of man-eating tribes bear any seed of reality?

"Shikamo," Christophe greeted as he reluctantly climbed the slope, slowly reaching out his hands with the palms face down. There was no reply, only hostile eyes piercing him like poisonous darts.

"I have a bad feeling about this, professor." Mackintyre half-whispered to Clayworth, pulling the tripod and bulky camera under his sweaty armpit closer to him.

"Please, people, have some faith. Nearly every tribe in the world uses attributes to make them look terrifying. It is only a matter of defense against other tribes, really." Clayworth brought the binoculars to his eyes and saw Christophe standing up there on the rim, gesturing to the natives who were gathered around him in a semi-circle.

"Professor, what is going on up there...?" Ms. Fairweather whimpered.

"By Jove!" Clayworth froze as he watched the scene on the rim take a turn for the worse. Christophe was suddenly dragged down to the ground by a handful of natives. Thrashing and kicking, Christophe tried to get away but two of the women straddled him and held him down. Like spiders attacking a defenseless insect, eight or nine men armed with machetes grabbed hold of his wrists and ankles while the two women sitting atop his chest started gouging out his eyeballs with twigs. The men started to hack off his arms and legs from his torso, and Christophe's scream echoed over the crater as blood gushed out of the jagged cuts. The machete-armed men then began to tear off large flaps of skin before sinking their teeth into the meaty orifices as if he were human steak tartar.

Clayworth dropped the binoculars and keeled over, vomiting over the cinder floor which sizzled fiercely as the bile splashed over it. "Run," he gargled.

Then the reeking slope came alive with the sound of cannibals charging them.

Mackintyre dropped his tripod and took two staggering steps backwards before he turned and ran; clutching his Dagor close to his chest as if it were a baby.

"Fire the rifle at them!" Ms. Fairweather yelled as she grabbed hold of Clayworth's shirt and quickly pulled him up. He began to plow onward the fastest he could with his bad leg. The surge of adrenaline luckily eradicated most of the pain and whipped him on to go faster, like a lame runaway horse.

Mackintyre was already out of sight when the cannibals reached the cinder floor, their feet scampering over the hot coal bed which sputtered and spit as though the crater were a giant frying pan.

Ms. Fairweather had reached the rim and was desperately pulling up Clayworth, who lagged behind. He panted as he fumbled to get up, but he kept slipping down as the boot on his bad leg refused to find a grip on the slippery ash. He craned his neck and saw one cannibal that was running much faster than his brethren, steadily closing the distance between them. Clayworth could now see that the mask he wore did not hail from a monkey, but was the loose face-skin flayed from one of their own.

Screams cannonaded inside Clayworth, whose sense of time and space suddenly warped from the immense horror.

On the opposite side of the crater, Christophe's dying wails had ceased, and the weakest of the cannibals now squatted around and feasted upon his flesh.

"Come on!" Ms. Fairweather begged with tears welling in her wide eyes. She tugged harder at Clayworth's shirt and let out a roar that made him snap out of his paralysis. He suddenly felt light as a feather and his body rolled smoothly over the rim and plopped onto the ground.

He picked up a rustle coming from behind as he got up on his knees. His survival instincts kicked in and he released the rifle from his back and peered over the edge. Not three yards down, he saw the masked cannibal clawing his way up the ashy hill. Their eyes locked for a brief moment. About fifteen yards behind were the rest of the cannibals, which Clayworth roughly estimated to be about twenty in number.

"Nitakula wewe!" the skin-masked cannibal snarled, creeping like a lizard.

"You filthy savage..." Clayworth said through gritted teeth. He aimed the rifle at the cannibal's head and squeezed the trigger at point blank range. The bullet shattered the cannibal's skull to pieces. In a bouquet of wet crimson flowers, his body toppled over and rolled backwards into the grave of ash.

The sharp gunshot that reverberated over the bowl-shaped crater startled Ms. Fairweather. Her hands pressed firmly at her cheeks and she cried hysterically. Clayworth slung the rifle over his back, grabbed his cane that laid next to him and sprang to his feet; cursing the fact that the rifle only held one bullet, and that the surplus ammunition was in Christophe's tent. He quickly limped over to Ms. Fairweather, who shoved her arm under his to speed up their escape through the blackened wasteland and into the dense thicket.

Not far behind them, the horde of enraged cannibals screeched as they rapidly ascended the slope like an army of starved, deranged primates.

14.
Orange Treetops

I could not have stayed a second longer. God knows I wanted to. But there were too many of those bloodthirsty savages. I would have been slain had I not fled from that horrid crater! Then this entire expedition would have been in vain. After all, it is I who have the photograph that will make us all legends. Damned fools! Why would they not listen to my warning in the first place?

Mackintyre was not sure how long he had wandered aimlessly through the oppressive thicket. Guessing from his sweat-drenched clothes that clung to his cooking body like a second skin, it was *too long.* This reasoning had repeated itself in his head like a psychotic mantra. Over and over again, he tried to find an ounce of sense in the nightmarish scene he had witnessed. He needed an equation to keep him from losing his guilt-ridden mind that steadily melted to a puddle of fear with each waterless minute.

"I will drink the entire sea when I reach that bloody beach," he quietly said to himself and brushed away some big drooping leaves – when something like a small cold hand suddenly ran up under the sleeve of his khaki shirt. He shrieked and dropped the camera. His heart jolted as he felt under his soaked shirt to frantically whisk off whatever critter was exploring him. His trembling hand met something wriggly and fast moving and he flinched from mental visuals. He pinched the thing and yanked it out with a shudder; his glassy eyes narrowing with loathe as he spotted the curious visitor crawling two feet away from him: a giant coppery-colored millipede that quickly disappeared under a lichenous root.

"This accursed jungle..." he muttered under his strained breath and scanned the immediate vegetation for more of the unwholesome creatures. Happy to find none, he worked up some saliva and picked up his camera to continue his hopeless drill through the exhausting ardor, wherein even the monkeys that jumped between the treetops seemed to mock him with their chattering laughter.

Another slow hour passed before Mackintyre suddenly noticed a wisp of curling smoke rising from what appeared to be a sheltered cove or glade further ahead. He stopped and crouched. His heart rate climbed and his temples began to throb in a march beat as he realized it was not nature's own design, but a primitive lair no doubt made by human hands.

A spiky wall encircled the sinister hideout, built using thorny weeds and branches, tied together by sinewy strings and some kind of greenish sap.

Mackintyre sat motionless and tried not to make a sound. Pearls of sweat dripped from his forehead to his parched lips, pretending that the salty little droplets were water as he caught them with his tongue. The pillar of smoke soon reached his olfactory sense and forced him out of his frozen stance as he regurgitated from the terrible stench of burnt hair and flesh that invaded his nostrils.

I am doomed, he thought as more bile rose in his throat, his red eyes locked on the vile shadowy lair.

No savages came rushing out. Mackintyre let out a sigh that carried a hundred suppressed breaths. His joints popped as he got up on his aching feet and sneaked over to the encampment. He did not find an entrance, nor did he want to. Instead, he cautiously peeked over the high wall that reached to his forehead.

First he registered a myriad of tools and weapons scattered on the stomped dirt-ground. Each one was primitive and seemed to hail from the Stone Age. Amid the disarray, by a dry berry bush, sat a generous pile of human feces infested with hungry flies. Mackintyre crinkled his nose and shot a cursory glance over the degenerate caravansary. His eyes wandered to the dying fireplace in the centre when a terror beyond his comprehension manifested itself. For over the faintly glowing logs, stringed to a tepee of long sticks, hung a half-eaten human infant – the poor baby's charred skin had the same crisp texture as a slowly roasted suckling pig.

"Oh, my God..." Mackintyre couldn't tear his eyes away from the inhumane act displayed before him. "Those wretched barbarians... they eat their own children." He wanted to scream and cry. His brain tried to steer him away, but his muscles did not obey. Without knowing why, he raised his camera and aimed its glass eye at that tableau of depravity, then squeezed the shutter-bulb and perpetuated the blasphemous scene. Deep inside, within the black chambers of his mental castle ruins, a coarse voice whispered about the fall of mankind.

Fffhuh!

"Ow!" Mackintyre winced from a sharp sting on the neck. In one swift motion his hand flew to his throat to snuff out the life of the attacking pest. An icy ripple coursed through him as he slowly yanked out, not a stinger, but a small dart. Pivoting, he expected to find one or more of the child-murdering savages, but saw no one.

A strong sudden wooziness suddenly came over him and within the fraction of a second, he couldn't feel his arms anymore. A never ending echo sounded from the camera as it hit a rock. Then his nervous system collapsed and his body, too, fell to the ground like a wilted flower. A coppery taste spread rapidly in his mouth and as he lay there, paralyzed and gradually dozing off, he saw several pink-eyed crimson-smeared faces, leering as they emerged from the orange-burst treetops up high. Mackintyre recognized one of them...

"It should not be far now." Ms. Fairweather wiped sweat from her upper lip and stared at the compass clutched in her trembling hand. "We pitched the camp South of the crater, am I right?"

"Yes," Clayworth panted, nodding. He cocked his ear and looked behind, making sure they were still ahead of their blood-thirsty pursuers.

"Now, we escaped from the crater in a Northwest direction, and we have kept moving Southeast for over an hour..." Ms. Fairweather's red drippy face suddenly grew hopeful. She squeezed Clayworth's tight shoulder and pointed toward a narrow path flanked by dry overhanging trees. "If I am not mistaking, the camp should be..." she paused, squinted and pointed ahead, "not a quarter of an hour that way!"

Despite the wonderful news, Clayworth was shot down. His leg was killing him, pulsating with a numbing pain that had spread to his lower abdomen. It felt as if a small fire was burning there. He forced a smile and his words came out raspy, "I must say, you are quite the explorer, but I am afraid you must walk the last bit alone. I am sorry, but I cannot move another inch. It hurts too much..." His face turned wry as he rubbed the calf of his bad leg. The brown pants he wore had now assumed a burgundy tone from sweat.

Ms. Fairweather's expression returned to worry. "You must be mad if you think I will leave you here alone with those fiends lurking in the perimeter. No, I simply refuse. We are so close now. I will carry you if necessary!" She stifled a weary chuckle at the image of Clayworth cradled in her arms like a toddler.

"Do not be foolish. Just go and get help. Dunkley and his crew, I am sure, must have rifles aboard the ship." Clayworth narrowed his eyes and wagged his finger. "Think wisely now, Ms. Fairweather. You are much faster without my dead weight. You will reach the camp in a jiffy while I hide here and rest. Now go." He waved his hand dismissively and hobbled over to a giant plant with maroon flowers that appeared in clusters at the top. He recalled Christophe referring to the curious plant as a "Giant Amber."

"Wait!" Ms. Fairweather hurried after Clayworth, who stopped and turned.

"What, now?" he muttered irritably and threw the rifle into the shrub.

She looked deeply into his blue eyes, and despite their pressing situation, hers were sparkling. "I love you, Richard," she whispered softly and shut her eyes; slowly leaning closer toward him.

Before he could answer, they had fallen into an ardent kiss. Clayworth, too, closed his eyes and felt as if he were tumbling down a warm stream to her abyss of love. He only wished for the current nightmare to be over. When it was, he was going to ask for her hand in marriage.

It would be a perfect new chapter! Clayworth thought as their kiss ended.

"I will be back with help quicker than you can say cat's pajamas," Ms. Fairweather joked. She blew him a kiss and began to jog down the tree-bordered trail. Next moment she was gone.

Clayworth crawled into the Giant Amber and let out a groan of relief/pain as he settled into a comfortable position. Soon, he became aware of the plant's strong gingery scent and instantly, he was taken back to the Christmases of his childhood, when his late mother used to bake him Ginger Biscuits. He rested his eyelids and massaged his fiery leg, picturing Ms. Fairweather and himself decorating a stout Christmas tree while snow flurried outside the frosty windows of their Tudor cottage somewhere on the Yorkshire moors. He smiled at the thought, and could even pick up lively laughter from their children, a boy and a girl, sitting by the crackling fire and writing wish lists to Father Christmas. The comforting scene lulled Clayworth into a momentary nap.

Ms. Fairweather's terrifying screams slapped him wide awake.

He shot right up and peered through the plant's thick foliage and saw Ms. Fairweather tearing back along the same path she had disappeared only minutes before. Confusion grew to horror when he saw that three loin-clothed men from the cannibal tribe were hunting her. One stalwart man with a grizzled beard wielded a long curved knife, and two adolescents followed close behind. One of the boys, the thinnest, had an overshot jaw and looked as though he had not even reached the mark of a teenager.

Clayworth ossified as Ms. Fairweather propelled herself toward the Giant Amber. Her terrified eyes stared straight at the bush and desperately pleaded for him to come to her rescue. Her hysterical squeals formed no audible words, but it sent a message clear enough to break his heart as he sat hiding there like a dastardly garden gnome.

Not two yards from the Giant Amber, the bearded savage caught up with her. He dropped his knife and grabbed her shirt with both hands, throwing her down on the undergrowth using the weight of his muscular body. She yelped as she fell head-first and landed badly on her chin.

Crack!

Spittle flew from her mouth as her jaws collided. Her lips burst like two ripe grapes and sent a spray of blood that colored the herbs and saplings red.

The two youths hurried to aid their leader. They tossed her over on her back and pinned down her thrashing arms and legs till they had her in a steady lock. The leader then positioned himself on top of her hips and reached for his knife. He cut open her soaked shirt and her bared glistening breasts jiggled as she tried to fend him off.

The boy who held her arms suddenly moved around so that he squatted on her throat, his knees upon her wrists. Her high-pitched protests dwindled to a mere gargle, after which he initiated a most sadistic duty. Forcing open her mouth with one hand, he used the other to fish out a plier-like tool from a leather pouch on his waist string. Working the metal gadget, he began to remove her teeth systematically, starting with her molars, and collected them in his pouch. Each tooth crunched and squeaked as it was torn from her bleeding gum.

The leader slashed her trousers open and pulled her underwear upward till they came off with a feisty snap. Ms. Fairweather bucked fiercely but was immediately pressed back down. She coughed blood as he drove his knife straight into her orange-tufted genital and ran it upwards, gutting her like a floundering fish. As her life-juice leaked out and slowly submerged her lapsed body in a glassy deep-red pool, the men – sans the denture collector – began to pull out her innards and feed themselves, chewing through the rubbery bowels as though they were stringed sausage.

This deranged and sinister act of rape-like murder, torture, and cannibalism, was over in the matter of minutes. About the same amount of time it had taken for Clayworth's soul to perish. Every iota of it was mercilessly exorcised from his bereft husk and manifested itself through tears. He could not hear his heart beat, nor conjure a single thought.

He considered himself a dead man.

In this vegetative state he watched from inside his green-leaf grotto as the three humanoid-shaped monsters sat together in the sunny glade and ate the inside of the woman he loved. Their hunger soon subsided and the bearded man hauled Ms. Fairweather's defiled corpse over his wide shoulder as if she were a shot buck. Prey.

They wandered off in the direction of the crater and passed Clayworth so closely, he could pick up the musty stench that came from the offal spilled out from her body and dragged along the low-growing weeds like a twenty-foot worm.

The dead man came alive by dusk...

15.
The Pig-Masked Cook

"'A powerful thought-provoking motif, with a vast depth and symbolic value that will remind every Briton of why we must spread enlightenment in the obscured corners of the world.' – That was the Royal Photographic Society's motivation as they handed over their prestigious Honorary Award for Photographic Criticism to young Mr. Finley Mackintyre. The renowned jury members unanimously voted for his controversial and much debated photograph, 'Devoured Life', a horrendous image of a murdered infant used as food for a cannibal tribe on a remote African island. I bet we will see plenty more of this up-and-coming talent in the near future—"

Mackintyre turned off the bulky radio unit he had installed in the study of his seaside mansion in Blackpool. He rose from the serpentine-framed Bergere Sette, stretched and had a sip of his chilled Brandy Alexander. He could not stop thinking about his newfound popularity that grew ever so rapidly since he made it out alive from the nightmarish meteorite island. Every newspaper around the globe had wanted to run his story along with some of his shocking photographs. This, of course, had started an insane bidding and landed him quite a handsome amount of money. He was living the dream.

A pleasant smell of broiled bacon suddenly found its way to his nostrils from the kitchen, where his cook was preparing his midday meal.

"Ah, luncheon. Jolly good." Mackintyre finished his drink and headed downstairs. Halfway down, something alarmed him. A maniacal oink was heard from the cookery. The hair-raising sound rapidly escalated into evil grunts which made him quicken his pace. He slammed open the door to the kitchen and was met by his cook wearing a pink apron and a pig's mask. He grunted and laughed at the same time, pointing at the reeking pan on which burnt pork was sizzling fiercely.

"What is the meaning of this?" Mackintyre demanded as he strode toward his employee, who had clearly lost his mind. Provoked, Mackintyre stared at the pan, at the crumpled rashers of bacon that were burning up, and then back at the insane cook. "Remove the pan, you are burning the bacon!"

The pig-masked cook did not reply. Instead, his demented giggle increased so much it was bouncing between the red-checkered walls, which dripped with grease.

"Did you hear me? You are burning the bacon! You are burning the bacon!" Mackintyre screamed at the top of his lungs, when the cook suddenly stopped laughing and lunged at him, sinking his fangs into his collar bone.

Screaming, Mackintyre jolted awake – and realized he was in Hell...

Awake, he found himself hanging from his collar bones in rusty hooks. He looked down and saw that his arms and legs were gone, cauterized, leaving him a swaying torso. Not an arms-length away, Ms. Fairweather hung in the same fashion. Her torso was picked clean, and though badly roasted, her head was still uneaten. She was staring back at him through gaping sockets; her crisp-skinned lips had reclined and formed a toothless 'O'.

As the thick smoke that rose from the glowing ground dissipated for a brief moment, Mackintyre could see the endless line of cannibals silhouetted against the dusky purple sky. Their feet hung over the edge of the high-level border where they sat filling their bellies with meat carved from Ms. Fairweather. It dawned on him that he was still on Earth. Still in Zanzibar. Back in the godforsaken crater he once escaped.

That was when Mackintyre became aware of the unyielding pain. His flickering eyes saw a million imps stab his skin cells with red-hot tridents, and slowly pour candle grease over his scorched tissue. As his tormented wails cannoned over the infernal basin, he did not register the sizzling footsteps behind him. In the next moment, the side of his stomach was sliced open with a machete, arresting his screams. Wet stringy intestines were brutally yanked from inside him and dropped onto the hot bed with an angry sputter.

Mackintyre's neck slackened and his head fell limp. The last image he ever captured was the steaming pyramid of his own frying guts.

16.
A New Life

The deserted camp looked spooky in the purple light of the sky. Wide-eyed, he quietly staggered through the soft sand and kicked crabs out of his way as he approached his tent. He peered desperately toward the icebreaker, whose faint silhouette drew itself against the mystifying light.

So close now...

All he needed now was his important notes, some ammunition, and his backpack to carry the many sample jars, including the unique, heavy object now resting in his pocket, before he could finally row out to the Blue Marlin that sat waiting for him out by the bay.

"The lifeboat!" he gasped in panic, his eyes immediately shooting toward the brink of the clucking water; relieved to find that his only ticket away from the island was still there.

His pulse raced as he used the rifle's shoulder stock to lift open the tent-door. The moment it came open he raised his weapon as something big and dark came at him. He swung the rifle in a wide arc at the attacker – his own flimsy shadow moving on the canvas wall.

He emitted a nervous sigh and quickly began to scrape together the necessary items into a backpack. His heart clattered like thundering horses. He hurried into Christophe's tent and was pleased to immediately spot the box of ammunition amid the late assistant's belongings. He grabbed a fistful of bullets and stuffed them into his pockets, making sure to place one in the rifle's chamber before he stashed the half-emptied box in the backpack.

With his cane in one hand and rifle in the other, he hobbled down to the lifeboat like a wounded soldier. He put the rifle on a seat and began pushing the bow. Tears welled up in his eyes at the wonderful sound of water clucking as the boat launched into the ocean. Clayworth clumsily stepped into the rocking vessel and began pushing the oars like there was no tomorrow.

With each stroke and with each yard he distanced himself from the cannibal island, his sanity strengthened.

The deep-violet sky had shifted to black when he reached Blue Marlin. Due to the growing darkness it was difficult to spot the steps welded onto the ship's hull. When he finally did, it took him less than a minute to climb aboard.

His boots and cane clunked against the bridge deck's metal floor as he hurried toward the captain's quarters. He figured that Dunkley and his crew were probably fast asleep at this late hour. His golden pocket watch showed a quarter to eleven. Further ahead, he could see Dunkley's stateroom window and was happy to find it glowing.

He barged through the sturdy mid-ship steel door and came into the narrow corridor that led to the gunwale. A centering staircase ascended to the decks below and across from that, a little bit ahead, was the captain's quarters. The large wooden door, decorated with a golden plaque, was ajar. Limping toward it, Clayworth contemplated how to break the outrageously strange and terrifying news. Where would he begin?

Just before he barged into the room, he glimpsed through the chink of the door, the familiar white-bearded contour of Dunkley who sat in a high back chair with his head resting on the desk. A bottle of brandy stood next to him, and Clayworth suspected the spirits was the culprit behind his noteworthy sleeping position.

"Captain, wake up!" Clayworth called as he knocked the door fully open and stormed inside. Upon entering the luxurious room, he first noticed that the captain's face was alarmingly pale. Then he saw the heap of entrails that bathed in a brook of blood around Dunkley's boots.

"No! No!" Clayworth's head spun as he faltered backwards and dropped his cane, which rattled to the floor.

Before he could pick it up, a naked tribal woman came crawling out from underneath the desk. She was soaked in blood and her mouth crammed with Dunkley's innards, which she chewed with difficulty. Her unhinged black eyes were locked on Clayworth as she rapidly rose to her feet and picked up a long bone with a dripping circular blade tied to it. She was about to charge him, but he managed to stagger out and slam the door shut.

Clayworth's eyes rolled madly in their sockets. He pressed his arms against the wood and flinched each time the cannibal-woman hacked her primitive axe into it. What should he do next? Was the woman the only cannibal aboard? If not, was the ship's crew still alive, fighting for their lives on the decks below? The questions tumbled inside his head and made him hover between hope and despair. He wanted to believe there was still a chance for freedom, even as splinters fell from the door as the axe cut through it from the other side.

During the struggle of holding back the door, Clayworth picked up the vague sound of bare feet against metal. They were coming fast. He craned his neck and reached for the rifle on his back, when a slender figure emerged from the staircase on the other side of the corridor. Pivoting, Clayworth pressed his backpack against the budging door and brought the rifle to his shoulder just as something sharp pierced his stomach and nailed him to the door.

Clayworth let out a grunt as his head slammed back against the battered door, now slowly pushing open with him attached to it like a human coat hanger. He could not breathe, and knew why the moment he looked down at the spear that jutted out from his left lung. A taste of iron spread in his mouth, a red cloud of blood sprayed the wall as he choked.

The spearman hesitantly crouch-walked toward him, as if fearing the rifle, while the cannibal-woman finally came through the doorway and bolted out into the corridor where she ran amok, howling with rage as she could not find her jailer, who was concealed by the door between them.

Pinned to the hard wood, Clayworth felt his life peter out. Selected scenes from his life flashed before him. He saw the pallid face of Death leer as it entered his black hazy vision.

"So... this is how my new life begins," Clayworth wheezed through blood-bubbling teeth, and enclosed his lips around the cold muzzle of the rifle...

ABOUT THE AUTHOR

Michael Faun writes exploitation and horror fiction. He's had nearly twenty short stories printed in various publications. His books include **Black Heart Metal Monster**, **SS Death Simulation**, **Deep Invaders #3**, its sequel: **X-haustpipe X-tasy #X**, and **Gillian's Marsh**. He lives with his wife, daughter, and three mice in a seedy town on the Swedish east coast. You can visit him online at **michaelfaun.wordpress.com** or contact him on Facebook: **facebook.com/michael.faun**

Printed in Great Britain
by Amazon

31326772R00038